Merry Christmas. Jan Bryant

TWO CORNERS
OF TIME

The Forest Ranger/
Two Sides of a Fence

Collection
BOOK FOUR

D1607920

By: Jan Bryant

PRESS

THE FOREST RANGER

D avid had moved to a new location for his job and found by accident a new way to deal, not only with animals, but with people, as well.

TWO SIDES OF A FENCE

S ometimes a fence can be good for keeping things out, but there are times that man will use evil to keep someone in. Danny is a man that has been on the both sides of the fence, a prison. We later see him having to prove his innocence all over again, as he adjusts to his new way of life.

THE FOREST RANGER

Chapter One

MY NEW HOME

O*h! What a gorgeous day this was going to be* was my first thought as I looked around the forest. In the sky there were sunrays of gold, hot pink, white, and so many more colors that I just cannot describe. There is a great beauty I see not only with my eyes but also with my heart! The gold color spreads out like a giant fan with fingertips trying to reach out as far as they possibly could touch. The beauty of the sky here has caught my breath, causing me to want to sit and take it all in. I'm sitting at a campfire; in my hand is a hot cup of coffee. It was hard to sip my coffee, for all I wanted to do was to drink in all the beauty of this new day and this new land. I have not only been a short while in Forestry; but I am now in a new town.

I just moved from a small town out west, so I am new to this area and could not believe such beauty could exist. There were things in my office that I needed to do, but my heart was having a hard time letting go of this outside world.

My name is David Williams. I am a third-year Forest Ranger. I did most of my time in Forestry in an old office, doing mostly paperwork. The times I did get out, the place was like a ghost town. There were not only a small number of people living there but the animals were also small in numbers. I am not sure if the lack of people was what caused the rough attitude of the town or if it was the people themselves.

When the Commander tells you are needed elsewhere and the transfer papers come in, you must go. I was dreading the move to my new town because I was not sure about the people or what I would really be doing. My new home of Featherton, Mississippi didn't seem to look any different than my old area on the map. However, finding out what Featherton, Mississippi in the Appalachian Mountains really was has turned out to be somewhat different. Finding out that there is about the same number of people did not bother me; it was the different attitude that I was glad to see. Oh, they seem to still have the roughness and a quick attitude, but I did not have to be afraid of most of them. I really think this place was more show than anything.

I went from stumps that were called trees and very little people, to a place where there are so many trees, plants, animals, hills, even mountains and well. The people were even a little nicer, except for the poachers. You still had to watch out for them wherever you went.

With all the extra wild life, I certainly do not have to go look for the animals. They seem to come out of the brushes when it comes to the time that I have to do the counting and tagging of all the new creatures that I find to catch. Today I must go to Eagle Valley. Of all the many valleys that I travel to, this is the most unique one of all. It gets its name from the numerous eagles that have made their homes there in the high cliffs close by. There is a special spot on one of the cliffs that I like to visit. Focusing, I can see for miles across the valley. You see only one or two houses on the floor of the valley. They are as small as ants. I sure would hate to fall; it is such a long way down. Someday I hope to be able to stay long enough to see a sunset from that cliff and to welcome the night in as I carry out my duties in that area.

There are days that are so peaceful, while other days, there is so much excitement going on all around that makes my days really long. It is those long days with all the joy and excitement that I hate to see come to an end.

Chapter Two

LOOKING BACK ON MEMORIES

Spring did not last long. In this hot summer season, it is hard to keep my shirts dry. Watching this day come to an end, I lay on my cot in the tent that once belonged to my dad. I caught myself thinking about some of the good times that my dad and I had as I grew up, like fishing or hunting. That was how I learned to love and respect nature. Dad meant for it to be a learning process, as well as a time of enjoyment for my family. The main thing that caught my attention was the beauty and innocence of nature. That was what caused me to get turned on to life in the forest. There was even one time that while we were hunting that I came across a nest that had fallen out of a tree. We had a bad storm a couple of days prior. Maybe that was what caused the nest to fall. It was at a time when there should have been a baby bird or animal in it, so I went to see if the nest was empty.

As I turned it over, there was a baby squirrel that must have been abandoned by its mother. As it slowly moved, I said to dad, "No telling how long the little fellow had been here." *I hope he will let me take it home to care for,* were my thoughts. It was limp as it lay there on the ground. It must not have eaten in several days. I guess I was around twelve or thirteen years old. My dad at first did not want me to take it home, but I convinced him that the little critter would starve to death without my help, so I scooped up the little creature in my hand. I wrapped him up in one of my extra shirts to keep him warm. I guess my dad would let this one slide, for he was not too disappointed in me as a hunter since he had seen me kill a twelve-point buck the winter before. That was when I realized that some things in life are meant for the table, but if we do not take care of what God has given us, then life could go off balance, and mankind could destroy what was meant for good.

Suddenly being hit in the face by a cold puff of wind quickly brought me back to reality. I really do not know why, but the place I chose for placing my tent to sleep in was under a tree that was about half the size of all the other trees surrounding me.   Now as I lay here in the darkness of the night, looking out the crack in my tent that was supposed to be the door, I began thinking about how tall and rugged the other trees were. They were so tall that I could hardly see the stars. With them being so big, they must be up in age. *I am not sure why I chose the smaller tree to cover and protect my tent, maybe if I needed to climb one because of a bear or another kind of animal I could get up that one a lot easier.* With that thought and a grin on my face, I laid down to go to sleep.

Because of being by myself, there were so many times that I would catch myself thinking, like what would I find when I am out away from the ranger tower or what kind of day tomorrow would be, since the night was passing fast. Lying on my cot, I was soon interrupted by the sound of creatures of the woods. Growing up, I had a recording of sounds made by different animals. The sounds intrigued me, leading me to mentally identify the sounds I was hearing now.

After being here for three months, it was time for a new season to start. I would find out soon how important life was to me. This twist of events would turn out to be the happiest time, as well as the saddest time, if that is possible, but things would have a good but unexpected ending.

Chapter Three

POACHERS

The warm season has come and gone. Soon the snow began to fall collecting on the trees and everything in its grasp. The snow soon piled up to great depth. The trees held snow in their branches and with any kind of noise made, there could be avalanches. Because I was by myself, I really had to be very careful when I went out to check my territory. I was told that since I was by myself, I would not have to go out as often until I got used to being here. When I did go out, there were times that I would find half-starved rabbits and would bring them back to my station. I would care for them until they had recovered, and then release them back into the wild. Now I see why my heart went out to these critters while I was growing up. My heart only continues for these animals and could hardly wait for winter to be over.

Now with the winter season finally coming to an end, there are many things that I had to watch for. The scariest things to find yourself in were being buried alive by an avalanche, falling in thawing-out ponds, or hungry wild animals suffering from lack of food. Not much to be scared of, you say? Everything and everyone has to look out for nature for what it can give to us, good or bad.

In my work, there were many different experiences that I had gone through in such a short time. Some were happy times of seeing the birth of newborn animals, and some were sad times of seeing unnecessary slaughter of animals. The slaughtering of the animals was the work of the poachers. Every time that I even thought of having to run across one, it made my stomach go into knots.

One day while trudging through the cold snow, I started thinking about some of the times that I had ran across what poachers had left behind. It is so sad to see how the poachers misuse the animals for only their hide for such little profit. Before I knew it, the thought became reality. There in the snow lay the carcass of a bobcat. As I examined it, I noticed that there on its right ear, a tag. That tag was to represent the protection for that animal, which was connected to my job. Yet, someone rejected that tag just for a few dollars they could get for the pelt. The cat had not been dead too long, just long enough to start smelling. Poachers usually treating animals this way come in two categories. They are people that have plenty of money or people without enough money, but both have the same goal in mind: greed for more money. That makes my blood want to boil.

As I looked upon this bobcat and other animals that were victimized, there are times that my heart wants to cry for the loss of that animal, out of compassion. As I dealt with the dead bobcat, the smell from the animal began to make me sick, but I knew I had to remove the tag before I could bury it. Pulling out my black book, I wrote down the number that was on the tag. Then I had to write down the reason for the loss of this wonderful creature. Once again looking at the tag, I placed it in the pocket of my black notebook. This was another of my responsibilities, to keep a record of information on all of the animals that I found dead, how they died, and if they had a tag.

I knew I needed to bury the cat, so I pulled out my shovel to start digging. The ground was hard from the cold snow. As I dug and dug on the hole, I started wondering if this female bobcat had any kittens. Just before I placed her ever so gently in her grave, I examined her. I noticed that she must have been too young to be a mother. I was relieved to know that there would not be a litter out there without a mother. With the loss of the cat, it made a terrible way for closing out the day before heading to my campground.

Back at camp, I noticed that there were a few stars in the sky. They were peeking through some clouds as to say I know how you feel, for I was tired, sad, and lonely in the dark of the night. Pulling up my warm sleeping bag and before I could get too far with my train of thoughts while lying on the cot, I fell asleep.

Chapter Four

FACING THE RIVER

When the weather decided to turn cold again, it was more than I could withstand. I was so used to a different form of weather. So I started sleeping in one of the Ranger stations. There was a solar-powered generator that operated the refrigerator, stove, a small heater, and my computer. Some other items that were in the station for me to use were a table, a much softer bed for me to sleep in, and a two-way radio. Except for the soft bed, I had not realized how much I liked sleeping under the stars.

Soon winter was to be over, but the snow still covered a great deal of the ground. There were times that I had to leave the station behind and go out to the wilderness for counting my animals. This was one of them. I knew I needed to go in the morning to check on the animals, for I would be out all day. The night was short. Before I knew it, I had to wake to face another day. The night had been extra cold since there were no clouds. Enjoying the night's rest, I did not want to get up. As I lay there hesitating from a short night, I once again pulled out my black book to read what I had written in it the day before.

Not having had the time to put the information into the computer, I decided I had better cipher what I had written earlier since it was done in such a hurry. I would write down notes of all my collected information that I needed to keep in that little black book, so when I returned to my office I could put it into my computer. I would not only put information about the animals into it, but also my closest thoughts in life.

The warmth of the covers gave me a second reason for not wanting to rise so quickly to do my duties. The covers did feel good, but the real reason for hesitating was knowing I would have to go down the river with its icy cold stream of water. There had been times that I would come to a close call in good weather with the rushing river, not being used to navigating in a canoe. This time, with the melting of the snow and ice, I knew the river would really be dangerous. The extra melting snow and ice would add depth and ruggedness to the river. I could not let the danger of the river keep me from doing my job. I knew that I could not let fear control me because fear can be more dangerous than the actual danger itself. When I signed up, I knew that I would encounter dangerous times. Convincing myself, I added a few warmer things to my suit of winter gear to meet the rugged Jacobs River.

What I had in mind was to check the beaver dams. One of the main rules that the Forest Rangers had when going down the river was to wear a life preserver. If you really want to know, it is the plain sensible thing to do, rule or no rule. While putting on my life preserver, I said a quick prayer, hoping that the prayer would take care of me with the wild raging waters that I would be competing against.

At first, dodging the rocks and swerving from side to side in my canoe seemed to be fun. The further I went down the river, the faster I went. Before I knew it, fear started to creep in. I tried to stay calm. I first felt it on the back of my neck, then it went down to my bones, as if my inner being knew something was about to happen. I wanted to try to get control of my feelings, but I would soon find out where those feelings would take me. No sooner had I felt those feelings when the waves of the white water rapids soon started splashing, reaching up to my shoulders, and then splashing over my head. Just about that time, the canoe was caught by rolling, fierce water, causing it to turn over. It started throwing out all of my belongings, as well as me into the thirty-two-degree water.

As I tried to swim toward the shore in the freezing cold water, I could feel my body wanting to shut down. I knew I had to reach the shore soon before it did just that. If I did make it to shore, I still had to start a fire and get my wet clothes off so that I could get dry and warm up my body to avoid freezing to death. I knew I had to keep my mind alert, so I started thinking about all the things that I knew I had to do once I got to shore. Trying to keep in mind was another of the first principals of forestry that we were taught. Still in the water, I turned my head, hoping to recognize the land where I was. Without any warning, the canoe came around hitting me on the left side of my head, causing everything in my sight to spin and then fade away.

Chapter Five

ANGEL OF MERCY?

Opening my eyes as I came to, I was wondering if I had gone to heaven or the other place. When most people experience a close call with death, they have that feeling and I was no different because that was my first thought. And there was my answer. My eyes began to focus on something leaning over me. Was it a young woman or an angel?

"Are you an angel?" I asked whoever leaning over me.

She just laughed. "I've been called a lot of things but certainly not that," my mystery woman said to me.

It turned out to be a young woman named Toni Barrow. Toni was about five and a half feet tall. She had short, curly blonde hair. She was dressed like she was about to go on a hunting expedition in Alaska.

"I am the one that pulled you out of the water," shared Toni.

I could hardly believe that she would be willing to enter that cold freezing water just to save me. She started to share with me at that time all she had done. As she was telling me all this, my head suddenly starting spinning and crashing so out I went. I was not out for too long, so she continued sharing with me on how she came about saving my life. As she told her story, this so-called angel soon turned into a bear. During the time she spoke, she took one look at my belongings strewn over the ground, and all she did was fuss.

In all the chaos, I tried to find out how she got there, but all she did was complain. It did not take me too long before it hit me who she was; she had this rude, snub nose, bear attitude of an ecologist. This time I wished that I could pass out again and not hear what she had to say. I had heard about them when I joined up with this forestry group. They said that there were a lot of the ecologists giving them trouble. About that time things began to sink in to what she was saying.

"There were visitors or campers that have a tendency to want to refuse to clean up the mess that they would leave behind after camping. Why? I do not know." She continued.

24

Because of her and the other ecologists fussing about it all the time, I knew right then and there that I had to do something to change things for the sake of the forestry division.

Chapter Six

NIGHTMARE OF DISCOVERY

As I tried to stand to gather my belongings, I discovered where part of the excruciating pain was coming from: my ankle. The pain was telling me that I must have sprained my ankle. Just about the time that I realized that I had hurt my ankle, the forest only seemed to start spinning around and around once again, causing my knees to buckle out from beneath me, taking me back to the ground. I knew right then that I must have received a concussion, as well, from the canoe hitting me in the head. With the confusion from my accident, my hurt head, and sprained ankle I just could not take it anymore, so I headed for the ground not willing to hear any more fussing. This time I got my second chance.

I found out, as I came to, that Toni had first taken care of me before she gathered what she could find of my belongings. She felt that I needed to rest due to all my injuries and all the confusion that we had gone through, and she made camp for us.

"Toni, I can't just sit here. Will you help me find a stick to use to walk with?" I asked. "I need to find something."

"I hate to say this, but you are not going anywhere. You need to sit right there, and I will help you find what you are looking for. Just tell me," insisted Toni.

As Toni brought things to me, I would go through them, looking for a certain item. "Did you lose something? What was it? Can I help you find it?" asked Toni.

"I need my radio." Now I was beginning to panic. I had a small radio that I would use to communicate with the main base or other rangers. That was the most precious thing that I had, and if I were to lose that, I would lose contact with the main ranger station. I continued to look. Sure enough, I had lost my most precious item, my radio. I was not sure how she would handle the news if I told her. I did not want her to panic, but I had no choice.

"I need to tell you that I have lost the radio, and I am not supposed to start reporting in to the tower for three more days, so no one would find out until then that I was in trouble," I shared unwillingly.

To have been able to come across Toni was a wonder, no, a miracle, because not too many people can be found in the woods during the wintertime. Matter of fact, only the people that you are likely to find are the bad guys, and they would rather let you die than to help you live.

With all the fussing Toni continued to do, I soon began to think that maybe it was better for a bad man to help me. I caught myself thinking, *Of all the different kinds of people in this world who could have come to rescue me, it had to be this rude, snub nose, bear attitude ecologist who did nothing but complain,* and did for the next two days. Oh, do not think that I did not appreciate the help she gave; I certainly did. She saved my life! It was because of how she acted that I was uncomfortable. About halfway through the second day, I could not take it anymore. I finally managed to convince Toni to help me gather my stuff together and for us to head out for the Ranger Tower. Running low on food and now no supplies except my black medical bag gave me every excuse in the book for not hanging around, but to help us head for Lookout Tower Number 3. It took most of the two days in camp for us to find the compass that had rolled under a log, and for me to recuperate enough from the concussion to walk. So as soon as we found it, we headed off in the easterly direction for that ten-mile hike. Since I was hurt, I knew that this would be a long and extra-hard trip. After sharing with Toni the importance of her not griping and to listen to what I would tell her, I think she finally got the idea that I was not too happy with all her complaining, and that was when things started changing drastically.

Chapter Seven

THE TRAIL

Going down the trail, I now saw that I had a new problem. Besides some snow still on some of the plants and ground, the brush was quite thick. The new problem was another item that Toni reassured me we had lost. It was the machete. Every once in a while during the summer season, a ranger would go down the trail and clear a pathway for everyone to use to make their way through the woods. With the snow and a little extra overgrowth left over from the summer made it even harder to travel. This time catching myself complaining about the lost machete, I guess if it had not been for my Old Faithful hunting knife that was about half the size of the machete strapped to my side, we really would be in trouble. That was when we both looked at each other and I realized what I was doing, griping. Soon we both let out a big laugh.

We managed to make about half of the ten-mile distance, when all of a sudden we heard a horrible cry. We stopped on the trail to continue to listen for it a few more minutes, hoping to hear the cry once more and to see if we could locate where the sound was coming from. "What could it be?" asked Toni. I motioned to her to be quiet. I had an idea what it was, but by keeping quiet for safety reasons, I was hoping that I was wrong. I certainly did not want to admit that the noise was coming from an injured wolf. That meant I would be the one caring for it. Being in my condition, I was not sure how I was going to do that. I also was not sure how Toni would react to a hurt wolf. Her being a girl, could mean a lot of things.

The reason I knew it was a wolf, was remembering once again about that recording I had as a youngster. I wanted to be prepared for the time that if I came across an animal hunting while making any kind of noise, I would know what was making the sound. Even if I was wrong, it may still need my help. About that time I had totally forgotten about being hurt. As the cry continued once again, we started down the trail hoping that whatever it was would not jump out at us.

We were now about three miles from the tower, when the cry led us off the trail about one hundred feet north through even thicker brush and more snow than what we had been walking through before. This time the noise turned into a whine. About that time I grabbed Toni's arm and pushed her to the ground. As I pulled back the snow-covered branch that was in front of us, there it was. It was a wolf that had stepped into a trap that a poacher had left. There was blood in the snow around the wolf. It looked like he had been chewing on his leg for a while hoping to get free, even if it meant walking on three legs for the rest of his life. "If I can get to him, I might be able to save his leg." I said in a whisper. Low and behold, I soon saw to my amazement another side of this so-called snub-nose, bear-attitude ecologist. It was like Toni had melted into someone else when she saw the wolf.

Chapter Eight

TO MY SURPRISE

Before I could stop her, she grabbed for my black bag that I was holding in my hand with all the medicine. She then headed out quickly from behind the bushes, then slowed down to see what she could do for the wounded creature. I really wanted to scream at her for this foolish act, but I was afraid by doing that; it would frighten the wolf and could cause major problems for Toni. With my hurt ankle, I was not as fast as she was. I knew that Toni's intentions of releasing the wolf were meant for good, but it could only mean trouble. In my mind's eye, I could see the wolf turn on her and hurt her after it was released. "Toni, no" I spoke in a soft whisper. "He will tear you to pieces if he gets out of there." Because of her earlier attitude, I knew she probably would not listen to me.

"He is only hurt; he won't hurt me," as if she knew something I didn't, Toni then sympathized with a smooth calm voice. Her now smooth voice did calm the male wolf down, so that she could help him. As she moved ever so slowly, she bent down to the ground to open the trap in hopes to release the animal; I could not believe my eyes. With each slow movement she made, I could hear Toni make a faint grunting sound from her throat, as if she was talking to him. This time she looked at the ground and not at the wolf. She told me later by not looking at the wolf while helping it, meant she was not challenging it with what she was doing. It helped to keep her safe. As I sat down with my sore ankle to observe her, I remembered about one of the mother dogs that I had when I was a boy. She would grunt to her pups as they lay down beside her to suckle when they would be a little rowdy. That mother dog also made the same grunting sound like she was talking to her pups.

There for a while, things were going good. It took a couple of tries before she could press hard enough to open the trap. At that time, I thought the wolf was going to bite her. I knew that if I yelled or made a fast movement, Toni was a goner. However, for some reason, something kept me still and not to say anything. It was as if someone or something got a hold of my mouth and would not let me speak. That was when I saw the wolf lean over to lick his poor wounded leg. The animal had to be in great pain. There was no telling how long he had been in the trap. I felt so sorry for the creature. I truly believe the wolf somehow knew she was trying to help him; that was why he did not attack her.

Since my job was to take care of the animals of the forest that was hurt, I knew I could not go any farther for now, no matter how bad off I felt. I now had a responsibility, but how dare she? She is doing my job of caring for the wolf, and I hate to admit it; she is doing a better job than I could have done. I just sat there watching her in amazement as I babied my own wound.

"Now there you are, Mr. Wolf. You just lay there and take it easy," softly spoke Toni compassionately. She then poured the disinfectant medicine on the wolf's foot with it not even squirming. Starting to wrap the paw, the wolf started gurgling at her, so Toni decided to just leave it alone. "Well, I guess this means we spend the night here?" asked Toni in a soft whisper. The day was just about to come to an end. "Yes, it looks like we have no choice," I said, really wishing that we could continue on. Here it was the third day, and we were so close to the tower. Toni then asked in a quiet voice, "Which compartment is the medicine for shots in? I want to make him more comfortable." Once again to my amazement, with a slight growl, he lay there and allowed Toni to give him a shot in the hip. Being so worried for Toni, I forgot about myself. I guess that was a good thing. Now lying there in my warm cover thinking of myself, all I could feel was a tired, sore, and hurting body that soon went to sleep.

I awoke the next day with this quick, yet horrifying flash of a picture in my mind that the wolf just might attack when he gains his strength, so we had better not turn our backs on it. With that feeling in mind, I jerked sitting up in time to see Toni fast asleep in her bedroll. I turned to see about the wolf. Sometime during the night the wolf must have felt better, for his presence was no more.

Chapter Nine

THE CONFESSION

Now that my responsibility was no more and Toni's work was done, we decided to head for the tower. As I tried to gather things together, Toni came over to me. She looked as if she had something on her mind. "Good morning. How was your night?" asked Toni. Then she tried to take a peek at the wound on my head. "It is good," I said in a little loud voice, while pulling away not willing to give her a peek of my wounded head.

By the new look on Toni's face, she must have had something that she wanted to share with me. Maybe she had something on her mind that I needed to know. As we began to eat our breakfast, she began. "Do you mind if we talk?" she asked. As I sat down on a big log, she began telling about a private part of her life that she had not shared with me before now. So as she pulled up an old loose stump close to me, she continued wearing that serious look on her face. Stopping to think how she wanted to say it, it was about her and her dad, along with all the wild animals in her life.

"I know you may think I was silly about trying to take care of the wolf," said Toni and she continued. "I want to share with you about me and my dad. This is why I became an ecologist. My dad told me one day that if there was only one thing in life that I needed to learn, it was that life was precious. My dad wanted me to learn that once life was gone, it could not be brought back, either in the world of mankind or in the world of animals."

As she shared with me, all my strange ideas that I had against her began to change. I finally started understanding why she was acting the way she did when we first met.

Lowering her head, she continued. "You see my mother died in childbirth. I was that child. My dad raised me, showing me how important life was and how life needed to be respected," shared Toni as she continued talking. "When I was a young teenager, I had many 'friends' in the wild. I had a bear cub named Junior and a raccoon named Suzy, with three baby raccoons. They each had a name, but that is not important now. I had rescued each of them when they were hurt. One day I found all my friends dead at different water holes. I also came across a mother cougar lying near her dead cub. She, too, was so far gone that whatever I did would not help her. I wanted to help, but before I could do anything for her, she was gone. You see someone had poisoned all the water holes within a two-mile radius of our place. Even Scooter, my dog must have gotten a drink from one of the bad water holes. I found my lifelong friend in the front yard. Before he died, he must have wanted to be back at our house. Poor thing, looking at his paws, he must have crawled all the way back home from where he was. I was told that the water holes were supposed to have been poisoned because of a wild dog killing off a great deal of the rancher's live-stock in the valley where I lived. However, it is hard to believe that people would be willing to jeopardize the lives of all the wild animals just for one dog. The irony of it all was whoever did it left a candy wrapper behind, leading us to the person." As she spoke, she could hardly hold back the tears. I now had a new vision about this "Angel of Mercy" that came my way in the nick of time.

Chapter Ten

DIAMOND IN THE RUFF

Heading the last short distance to the tower, I realized here that Toni, who once reminded me of a piece of coal, now because of the pressures of life, had turned into a jewel, a diamond. Now my snobby, snub-nose, ecologist took on a whole new look. Yes, I will even admit that she took pretty good care of me while we were in the forest. I believe she meant well with all her fussing, but now she can put it to work, by using it in a way of helping others and all the wildlife in the woods. You see, we needed two persons for the department for the tower to see to the animals. There was a job opening available for someone just like her. With this thought in mind, I felt that she could use her heart of gold to take care of all the hurt animals that we find, too.

As we approached the tower, I noticed how it sure looked wonderful for just being a metal building. I had enough excitement and tragedy of hurts to last a life-time. That was when I decided to ask her my question.

"Toni, want a job?" I asked.

"A job?" questioned Toni, "You've got to be kidding."

"No, I mean, yes, we could use your talent with all the creatures of the woods, and besides you work almost as well as I do. I saw how you handled that wolf, and you do have a lot of caring to share. We happen to have an opening. So, how about it?" I asked.

"Yes," agreed Toni, surprisingly.

I guess I did not want to admit it, she was actually better than I was in our field of work, since she was the one who had to rescue me.

My Dad taught me a lot about life; but I think Toni taught me just as much, dealing with the wild creatures of the woods. That is why I wanted her help.

The End

TWO SIDES OF A FENCE

Chapter One

THE FIRST SIDE OF THE FENCE

When people talk about two sides to a coin, they mean there are two stories or two different meanings to be considered. Well, life can be like that, too. Life can be a fence that has two sides; each side of the fence can tell a story. However, there are times that a story can be mistaken in the wrong way or even be totally misunderstood. Let's see that today. For many years, while growing up, there was a fence around our front yard. That fence was a means of protection for my family and me that did not allow unwanted people onto our property.

As the years have gone by, I now see how a fence can be used in two total different ways. There are times that people like to invade your privacy to steal your possessions; with a fence, they can be kept out. Another way may not be quite so pleasant. The unpleasant way would be for holding people in, like a prison. The reason it was be so unpleasant to me was because I was the one that was being held in against my will behind this fence. There are times that people are put in prison because they deserve it. However, there are times when people, like myself, are put there due to injustice. Yes, I was charged with a crime of robbery that I did not commit, taking close to six years of my life away from me that I will never get back.

As my final days in captivity come to a close, I mentally wanted to move forward to this new day of February 10, when I am about to be exposed to a world that I had not been part of for so long. You see, I, Danny Blanchard, had been behind that chain-link fence that would not let me out for six long years. To me, that was a lifetime.

When other inmates would go outside in the court-yard of the prison, using their time for their conveyance, I felt differently. I would catch myself standing there at the outer fence, looking out beyond the twisted wire to the blades of grass and the tree line, where a world that I once knew existed. I am not sure what I was thinking about; all I knew was that I did not want to be in this pit. Life was unfair to me. My family and I did not get along, and I really feel I was there because my family wanted me out of their way so that they could do some unlawful things themselves. The only way to do that they lied by trumping up a charge, of stealing a large sum of money from them, so that it would get me out of their way to do what they had in mind.

The fear of knowing that I would be released only added more fear to not knowing what I should expect to see as I crossed through that gate and over the imaginary line to freedom. Each day, waiting for that special day to come, was spent out on the patio. While in my daze looking out, the horrifying fear would cause my fingers to intertwine the chain-links with a strong grasp, not knowing if they would or would not let go. Each time, I had someone to come and peel my fingers off the wire so I could return inside. Being outside was the only way to feel halfway free, as I waited to be fully free, so I hated to have to go back inside.

It was not fair for the guards to constantly remind me each day of the things that changed so much while I was in prison. It could make a person want to give up trying and want to stay behind the fences. For the last five years, life has been a nightmare. I was hoping that one day I would wake up and find out that this was all a bad dream, but it never did, for it was real.

Somehow, I did manage to win the battle over that feeling. With that special day here, I can now look back and think about it. I do remember calling at times on the God that my mother had shared with me as I grew up. If I were only willing to let him help me now, I know he would do it. He was the one that I feel who helped get me out of here. He really did come through to help me.

With all the fear I had, I was to find out that really not too much changed in this world while I was gone. However, what did change were things that would affect me directly. I knew, because of the circumstances, that I would probably never see my brother, my ex-wife, or son ever again. I was going to have to be the one to adjust completely. All I really wanted to do was to forget all the things that I went through, the way I was treated in jail, and the thoughts that other people put into my head. Now that the time had come for me to be set free. I hoped that I would be able to put everything behind me.

Before the prison would let someone out, they had a job and a home lined up for them. I noticed in my files that a little town called Pottersville in this state of Arkansas was listed. I guess that was where my mother had moved to for me to come out of prison. I knew I was going to have to start my life all over somewhere. Really not knowing the place to start or the direction to go, I decided to do the best with what I had. As I walked through that final prison gate to freedom, I could only remember the words that rang in my ears.

The words of being told to, "Behave yourself, be good, and don't get into any more trouble," sounded really strange coming from the people in charge of the ward. To the guards, the words really don't mean much. The guards in charge of the prison only say those words out of habit, but to them the words really had no meaning; they were just words. Because of knowing I was innocent, and having to prove that to everyone who comes along will be hard to do. In my heart, I know that I have to forgive my family for putting me there, not really understanding why, except for possible greed. The new road I was to travel on now would be a new road, and God would have to show me the way.

While I was in prison, my mother had been sending me some money each month. I knew she was in poor health, but I did not know how badly off she really was. The money she sent for me to buy my writing paper, stamps, soap, and other needed items while I was there stopped about a month before I was released. Just before I was to walk out, I was told about my mother's death. The name of Mrs. Martha A. Blanchard would never exist again on mail or a box.

Chapter Two

A DESTINATION OF UNCERTAINTY

It was early in the morning as I walked up the steps of the bus. I was now about to see the second side of this fence. On this bus to my new destination of uncertainty, the one thing that I really wanted to be was free, totally free. Free to do the things I wanted to do and to go to the places I chose to go. Being free meant no more men following me around with guns, looking over my shoulder. Freedom also meant that I could have most of my wants fulfilled once again that I used to take for granted, like the simple desire to taste a cold orange or grape drink. That means I could make the choice for myself; no one would be making the choices for me. In prison, there was no such a thing as a cold drink, for they were always hot. Because of being in prison, I know that I will never totally be free, but I will certainly be freer than while I was in there.

The bus drive was long, but not far enough away from that nightmare of a place. As the bus that I was on pulled up to the drop-off station in that small town of Pottersville, Arkansas, I was soon brought back to reality with a hard jolt of the brakes. Of all the times that I was faced with the bullies in prison, I knew how to handle them; yet, I would soon meet the other kind of people in this world. I was not sure about whom I would face in the little town of Pottersville; I just knew that they would not be the same. With the remaining money in my account, my ticket could only take me that far with some extra for food. I am not sure why this town was chosen for me since my mother was gone. I guess, agreeing to go there, I just wanted something a little different than what I was used to living in. Hoping that it would help ease the butterflies in my stomach, I took a deep breath before walking out the door of the bus. As I stood there in the street collecting my thoughts, the bus began to pull away. It left me standing in the middle of the street.

As I looked down the street one way, I noticed at the end of the road, there was a tower with a clock that was finishing striking five in the afternoon. At the other end of town, there was a cafe called Suzy's Road House. I was hoping that maybe someone there could help lead me to where I was to go work. Soon, the thought came to my mind; I could finally get that ice-cold drink that I had been wanting for so long. All of a sudden my thoughts were interrupted when an old truck zoomed past me, coming close to hitting me. I then realized that if I did not get out of the road soon, someone would run me down, and for sure all my problems would be over.

As I slowly walked up to the door of the cafe, I got all my thoughts together and knew what I had to do and say. As I opened the door, it seemed to have an unusual squeak. It was not a scary squeak at all. As a matter of fact, I believe it was trying to say welcome; come on in. When I walked through the welcoming door into the cafe, there were all kinds of people there. I noticed that some were old, some were young, and there were even some of different races. Some of the people were there for buying food, like a meal. Others were there just to visit with their friends. I was there in hopes of finding the job that Warden Johnson had set up for me. Most of my experience was working on a farm with animals and equipment; therefore, he thought that would be best for me. Since most people seem to like to meet at the café, I was hoping this would be the most likely place, being the information center of the town, but what would I find?

I decided that the warden was right; ranching would be the best for me. Being that I was indoors for so long at the prison, I am not sure if I could take being inside of a building all day. The few times that helped to keep my sanity, was when they would let me go out to work in the fields to process the food that they were growing or to do some form of a repair job on the equipment. Another reason that I wanted to go and work on a ranch is that I have a great love and respect for animals. Not too many people have seen that side of me. I seem to get along better with animals than I do with people.

As I walked across the floor in the café, I felt everyone's eyes turned to look at me. With everyone staring at me, all I wanted to do was leave, but if I was going to get the work promised to me, I knew I had to be more patient with people and myself. I noticed an empty bar stool at the counter, so I sat down to see what they had on the menu to eat. I could tell the two waitresses were having a little talk, was it about who was going to wait on me? Soon one of the waitresses came over to me for an order. I first asked for that long-awaited drink. "May I have a cold drink, please" I asked. "What kind would you like," the waitress asked? "Just any kind, orange or grape, whatever you have will be fine. As long as it is cold," I shared. "Hey! You're new in town. Are you the one that just got off the bus," the waitress asked? We don't get too many newcomers in town. By the way, my name is Charlotte Greene." She announced. "It's nice to meet you, I'm Danny — Danny Blanchard." As I introduced myself, I thought to myself, *how quiet this little town seems to be.* It seems to be a good place that my parole officer chose.

As she reached for my cold drink in the cooler, I began to ask Charlotte about the ranch. "Charlotte, do you know where the Chandler Ranch is?" If she knew where the Chandler Ranch was, then it should be easy to find. I tried to listen to what she had to say, as I thanked her for the drink putting the cold bottle of orange drink up to my dry lips. The feeling carried me away to the point that Charlotte had to bring me back to reality. "Sir! Sir! Yes, I know where the Chandler Ranch is."

After Charlotte got my attention, she then shared with me where it was and what forms of work that the ranch does. She said, "You need to talk to a Mrs. Amanda Chandler. She is a widowed lady that owns about 3,500 acres around here. Since Charlotte did not talk too highly of her, well, it was not what she said, but how she said it, it made me a little skeptical about wanting the job. I continued to sit there, taking in what she was saying and all the flavors of goodness from my drink, until the last drop passed over my dry, parched throat, hitting my stomach. After I finished my orange drink, I asked for another one. This time I wanted the grape and the Wall Special of a hamburger and fries for a meal. *Now that I am free, I can ask for another drink without having to get permission.* With the thought, a slight smile came up on my face.

While enjoying my drink, Mr. Crumbly, an easy-going white man, who was short, stubby, bald-headed, and up in age, came up to me as he was heading to pay for his meal. Turning, he mentioned to me that he had overheard my conversation with Charlotte about a job. He said that he would be heading over in Mrs. Chandler's direction as soon as he paid for his meal and would be willing to take me. I had no way of getting there, and I was new in the area. It was like God had come through for me so many times, and this would not be the last time, either. I decided to take him up on his offer. Before I could finish my meal he was out the door. Having to leave half of it behind, I hurried out the door. With a grin on my face, I recognized his old truck as the one almost running me down.

Well, what Mr. Crumbly said and did were two different things. Yes, he ended up going in her direction, but what he forgot to say was that he was not going all the way. He ended up dropping me off about two miles short of her house. He said that it would be only a short walk down her driveway to her house. If that was a short walk, I'd hate to see a long walk. That so-called short walk would be to me the second longest and loneliest walk that I would ever take. The first longest and loneliest walk was the walk out of prison because of not knowing where it would take me.

Not having had much exercise and carrying a small bundle of things, the walk was tiresome. After stopping to catch my breath several times, I came to a clump of trees. As I came around the trees, there it was. Everything was like a picture, especially with the sun about to go down. As you looked from your right to your left, there was the main corral for most of the horse breaking, and then there were the main barn and more corrals and holding pens, which are next to where the bunkhouse was. This is where all the hired hands were staying and where my new home would be, if I were hired.

Then there were the open grounds that were followed up with a western-style home of true and great character and beauty. The house stood on a hill that overlooks a small valley. It was like walking into another world as I crossed over a small bridge. As I stopped to look at the house, I noticed that the designer made it fit in with the surroundings of the land. "*Now that is real talent,*" I thought out loud. For the house to have such beauty, the designer must have displayed what was in his heart. While I walked toward the house, I noticed that there were two driveways up to the house. There is one that led up to the front door and another one that went to the back of the house.

As I continued walking toward the front door, I tried to imagine what the owner of the house would look like. Ringing the doorbell, I continued to try to come up with an idea, but before I could, the front door began to open. There before my very eyes was this beautiful creature. Was this Mrs. Chandler? She had long black hair with fair complexion. I wanted to say that she could not have been more than forty-five by what I had heard about her, but she looked much older. Was that from all her troubles she had in life? As she stood there, she stood with dignity. Without any warning, she opened her mouth to inquire about my visit.

In about two seconds with her attitude of speaking, all the image of her great beauty seemed to quickly fade away. All she seemed to want to do was complain, fuss, and to show an unruly attitude. Her voice soon was bringing back the voices from prison and their harshness with the feelings of fear once again. The idea to run hit me again, but I knew I needed to work somewhere, so I decided to hang in there once again and see what would come about. When she found out that I was the one for hire, she told me my place to enter the house was through the back door, but this time she would let me in the front door.

As I introduced myself, I entered the house into this great open room. As I passed by some other rooms, I was able to see all the different forms of awards and the many ribbons that anyone person could imagine having. These awards began in the entryway, stretching all through the main part of the house. Along with the awards were pictures of a man with different horses being displayed in small cases. They were placed along the walls of several hallways. I even noticed there were plenty of pictures and awards in one of the small rooms that we went by. I assumed most of the pictures and awards belonged to her husband, since there were no pictures of her. There are also several large glass cases of awards that someone had received while doing events like riding, roping, and steer wrestling. The thought, *it must have taken a longtime to get these awards,* went through my mind as we continued to walk through the house. We went by several rooms that were full of pictures, to a room that had no pictures, no, not even one. In the room with no pictures, Mrs. Chandler and I sat down while she gave me an interview.

No sooner did we get started talking, my interview had come to a quick close. I was sharing with her about the many places where I had worked and what kind of equipment I had worked with in the past. With her hand, she abruptly cut me off, telling me what my work on her ranch would consist of. She then stood, with no inclination that our conversation was to be over, she started to leave the room pointing in a direction, leaving me to find my own way out of the house. As she was about to walk through the doorway she made her closure of our conversation by sharing with me that she knew I would be coming because a warden, Mr. Johnson of the prison had notified her. I was to find her Foreman Pedro and start my duties the next day. I wanted to share my side of the story, but she cut me off so quickly, that I did not even get the chance to tell her. So, for most of the time, we saw very little of each other, keeping my secret safe for now, or was it really a secret?

Chapter Three

MY NEW BEGINNING

My parole officer, Mrs. Randi Bains, "The Hammer Hatchet," as the prisoners refer to her, was aware of where I was and what I was doing. It seemed like every time she came, I was in town doing errands for Mrs. Chandler or the ranch, so that was where we ended up meeting. I did not plan it that way, but I certainly was glad. Because of my parole officer knowing the attitude of Mrs. Chandler continues to express, Mrs. Bains didn't mind having our meetings in town each time. Somehow Mrs. Bains always gave me a good report, so I guess she was watching me.

For the three months that I have been here, everything was going pretty good. I guess I was glad that Mrs. Chandler and I saw very little of each other. Amanda, or should I say Mrs. Chandler, could be difficult at times, but as long as she does her thing and lets me do mine, I will not complain. She seems so strange. Was she always like that? She seemed not to like being with people, but neither do I. I guess I need to watch who I call strange. Thanks to Foreman Pedro; he showed me the ropes and was there when I needed him.

The real thing where Mrs. Chandler and I differ is when it comes to the animals. When I see her riding her horses, it is obvious that she has no compassion for them. Mrs. Chandler has this outstanding white horse. He is over seventeen and half hands high. His name is Lucky Seven. One day, I was out in the pasture, mending fences, when she and Lucky Seven rode by without a word to me. I do believe that with the devotion that the horse has for its master, he would be willing to give his life for her if it were necessary.

Yet, I could not believe what my eyes were seeing. I guess the horse was not going fast enough for all she did was beat on the horse. She would whip it over and over, yelling at it. No matter how fast he was going, I guess she was not happy. If I had not been in the middle of my work or knew that it would jeopardize my job, I would have given her a piece of my mind, as I felt she deserved. However, that was one of the first things in a prison that I had to learn, to keep to myself. If you did not learn to keep your thoughts to yourself, you were in trouble. When any one of her horses got hurt, she would act like she really did not care.

I wonder what could have happened to cause this lady of great beauty, to turn her heart so ice cold and cruel. It is a good thing that I am here. I know that I needed a job and a place to live, but these animals have no one to truly be loved by, understand, and care for them like I do.

Chapter Four

A SUMMERTIME VISITOR

As the cool spring flowers faded away and the summer flowers were just starting to bloom, I could tell that something different was about to take place on the ranch. Things were humming about like a beehive. The maid, Mary Beth, was running around like there might be someone coming. The cooks were conversing about all the different new meals that were to take place in the house for Mrs. Chandler. With things humming around the house, my curiosity was aroused.

I asked the hired hands, but no one wanted to volunteer any information. Finally I was able to convince Pedro to let me know what was about to take place. "Jill, Mrs. Chandler's daughter, will be coming home for the summer," shared Pedro.

"Her daughter? I did not know she had a daughter." *I knew I should have told Mrs. Chandler,* in a half voice, not realizing that she may have already known. I questioned myself: *But I saw no pictures.*

Still confused, not quite hearing or more like understanding what I was trying to say, he said, "Yes, she does have a daughter. What do you mean by, I should have told her?" Pedro soon became confused now and wanted to question me. I guess I said it too loud even under my breath.

"Never mind; just tell me about her," I demanded.

"She has been off at school in Utah. She is now thirteen years old, and she has only a few pictures, which are in another room. Unless you knew where they were, you would not know about them," said Pedro. "I have been here for five years. She went off to school shortly before I was hired. I did not know about her or the pictures for about six months when she came home for the first time."

"If she is so young, then why is she so far away from home?" I asked *hoping to be wrong.* "Mrs. Chandler and her daughter do not get along very well. Then when Mr. Chandler was killed, things got worse, I was told. It is so sad to see the two of them together. All they did was fight," sadly confessed Pedro. "Mr. Chandler was killed shortly before I came to work as foreman. They say his horse fell on him."

"Do you know which horse?" I asked Pedro.

That was when Pedro told me, "They say it was Lucky Seven."

Chapter Five

THE SECRET

For the last two days, the ranch seemed to only hum with an uneasy feeling. I wanted to go to Mrs. Chandler and tell her my side of the situation and see if she still wanted me here when her daughter came for a visit. No matter how hard I looked for Mrs. Chandler, she was not to be found. About nine in the morning on this third day, I was out in one of the corrals working with the horse, "Scooter," with his lead rope. All of a sudden, I noticed a large rolling puff of what looked like smoke or maybe a cloud of dust in the air. If it was a cloud of dust, it seemed to be coming our way. The longer I looked, the more I could see that it was dust coming from a taxi. The yellow taxi driver seemed to be in a hurry, causing dust clouds as he drove up to the house. I see now that it could be too late.

The name on the taxi read "Yellow Cab Company." I stopped what I was doing to see who it could be. Soon out stepped a tall, blonde, slender girl. What she had on was high-class clothing. As she stood beside the taxi, the driver managed to get out three sets of luggage. Placing them on the ground ever so quickly, the driver collected his pay from the slender girl and was off. After paying the taxi driver, he drove off, leaving her in a cloud of dust. Fanning her way out of the dust, she then turned to look my way.

I quickly dropped down behind a pile of hay so that she would not see me. Her looking in my direction of the barns was as if to be examining something that she had not seen for a long time. Dusting off her skirt while holding her suitcases, she then hesitated oh so slightly before going up the sidewalk to the house. A few steps from the front door, she paused again before reaching for the knob. I wondered what was going through her mind. At that moment, she looked almost lost, as I felt the day I got out of prison. I read her actions as if she did not want to go into the house, but she had no choice.

No one seemed to want to talk about Mrs. Chandler or her daughter, since Jill was not there very often. They were so hush, hush about it the whole time; yet, I am sure they did because they are all humans. Here

I was hoping that my past was just that, the past, but it looks like my secret may have to come out. I had no choice but to tell someone. Just about that time my stomach jumped into my throat. Not knowing who to tell, I decided to share my secret with Pedro. I felt that I could trust Pedro not to go around telling everyone in town what my life had been about. Not only that, but Pedro has become my best friend. "Pedro, can I talk to you about something?" I asked.

"Ah, sure. Let's go outside. It is too noisy in here," suggested Pedro.

"I did not know that Mrs. Chandler had a daughter," as I started to share with him.

"I think she is just a little too young for you," Pedro teasingly said.

"No, that is not it. When Mrs. Chandler hired me, she did not tell me that she had a daughter."

"What would her having a daughter have to do with you getting or not getting the job?" asked Pedro.

"Just hear me out, please," I demanded!

"Have you seen the lady that I have been meeting in town at the park? She is my parole officer?" I shared. "I was accused of stealing money from my family, but I did not do it. I think they only wanted me out of the way so they could do something illegal. I had met some new guys who I thought were my friends, too. As time went on, all my friends, my wife, and my kid wanted to do was to sell drugs, which I tried to stop. They knew how I felt about drugs. That was the only way of getting rid of me, I guess.

By this time I wanted to find a small rock to crawl under. Pedro looked at the ground, then he looked up, not really knowing what to tell Jim. So Pedro just blurted it out. "She knows, Mrs. Chandler, she know about your prison record, but we weren't sure what you were accused of. Jill will be here only two months and twice a year, if that often. You are too good of a worker to let something like this interfere."

Trying to think, "But two months is a long time." I spoke. "My parole officer's next visit is to be here on the ranch. No telling when that might be. What if she shows up while Jill is here? I could go back to prison," I didn't know if that really was so, but I did not want to take the chance. I certainly did not want that. You've got to help me," I begged.

"Okay! Okay calm down," reassured Pedro. So I gave Pedro some time to think, hoping that he could come up with a plan. Pedro really did try to come up with a plan, but all I could do was to take each day as it came.

The next morning I was out seeing to a horse in one of the eastern corrals, when I noticed that things seemed to be moving earlier and faster than usual over at the house, when in the past it took a long time for things to start moving. As the front door opened, out came Jill. I tried my best to dodge her. I did so well at keeping my distance for the last several weeks. I really do not want to get the girl in trouble or myself. I am just not sure if I can do it again today or for how long I can keep it up. There was something so different about Jill, compared to her mother. Jill seems to enjoy ranch work. She would hunt out Steve and Pedro to help each day with what they had to do. I just was not sure how I was going to help her get involved with working on the ranch during her stay. Her face showed joy of wanting to be part of what was going on around here, where her mother only came outside when she had to. Mrs. Chandler would leave all the work up to the hired hands as if she never wanted to dirty up her own hands.

Chapter Six

THE FORGOTTEN LETTERS

It was now at the end of my fourth month here, and Jill had been here for almost a week. At first, the time dragged by slowly. As I worked on the ranch and finished with one part of my work, it is almost time to redo it all over again. I kept myself as busy as I could. The work that I did was good therapy for me. By doing just that, by the end of the day I barely could put one foot in front of each other to make it to the bunkhouse. As the weekends arrived, the guys liked to do their thing of going to town for the movies or to do something fun. Each Saturday, I would find an excuse not to go to town. I usually would tell them that I was too tired and wanted to stay on the ranch.

Tonight one of the workers, Frank, decided not to go to town, too. As I was dragging myself over to the bed to gather my soap and towel for a hot, relaxing shower,

Frank stopped me in my tracks by asking to borrow a pen. "Hey Danny, you got a pen? I want to write my girl," asked Frank.

"Sure do. Hang in there and I'll get it for you," I said. While looking for the pen, Frank tried to tell me where his girlfriend lived and what her name was, but all I could think about was getting in the hot shower to take care of my weary body. I went over to my bunk, laying my stuff down, I reached under my bed to get a small duffle bag that I had purchased shortly after I got out of prison. As I sat down on my bed to open the bag, I quickly unzipped one of the small compartments to get out a pen. There were the letters that I had placed in a location where I had succeeded in forgetting them until now. These were the letters that I had written to Mom the last month I was there in prison.

I first pulled out the pen and tossed it to Frank. As I sat there, I then pulled out the small pile of letters, trying to decide what to do with them now that Mom is gone. Because I did care a great deal for my mother, I wrote to her just about every week. I had managed to write several letters to my mother just before I was to be released.

I began to fade, looking out the window and thinking about that day. As I was about to leave, the warden had me to go to the collection cage. That was where you left behind all of your belongings when they checked you into prison. The officer in charge had my things in a brown envelope. He had me open and pour all of its contents out onto a table to see if everything I had before was still there. I began to thumb through what was there.

On the table laid my unfaithful watch for keeping time. I started to throw it away since I was used to not having one on my wrist. Then thinking twice, I decided having some form of a timekeeper was better than not knowing what time it could be at all, so I placed it on my wrist. I then noticed lying on the table the ring that my dad had given me just before he died. That had been several years before I was put in jail. As I picked it up to put it on my finger, I stopped to look at it once more. It had seemed forever that I had last seen it.

There was a receipt or two of no importance next to my wallet. I knew that there was not much in the wallet, just a few bucks and the pictures of my ex-wife and son. Now that I would never get see my family again, I took the picture of them out along with the unnecessary receipts and let them all slowly fall from my hand into a trash can next to where I was standing. The only remaining item of the table were my letters to mother.

Being surprised that they were not mailed, I noticed that they had a little wear and tear, as if they had been tossed around on someone's desk as though they were of no importance. Picking them up, I also noticed that there was a small notation on front of each letter as I thumbed quickly through them. The notation said, "Deceased, unable to mail. Please return to sender."

That was when I was told that my mother had passed away. I know now why I did not get a response from her. As I gathered my things, I almost had no reason to leave. The prison warden had refused to tell me of her death earlier, so now I really did not have anything to live for. They thought that I had no business going to her funeral since I was behind bars.

Sitting here, back in the bunkhouse, holding the pile of letters, a strange feeling came over me, and I had to read them. For some reason, the need was so strong that I could not resist it. I hoped that if I read only one of the letters, the feeling would go away. Maybe it was to put closure on that part of my life. So my shower was going to have to wait. It was as if there was a link to those letters, and it had to be broken. It seemed like the line that I remembered the most using was when I told her that I could hardly wait until I got out so that I could take care of my dear sweet mother. She was my inspiration, my heart's desire, and my will to stay alive so that I could take care of her.

Now that I have my freedom, my mother has left me behind in this world that I wish not to be a part of. As I finished reading a couple of letters, I felt a heavy piece of the burden leave my shoulders, breaking the tie of needing to read anymore, as well as to keep them.

As I put the letters that I read back into the envelopes, I retied the small bundle together. I noticed off to the right of Frank's bunk was a small trash basket. I soon got up and walked over to it, where I let my thoughts, my life, and my previous world slip out of my hand, down to the bottom of the basket, with a thud. *Now for that hot shower* I thought to myself.

Chapter Seven

THE MEETING

A s a new day dawned, it never failed; my watch seemed to have a mind of its own, causing it to run behind. When my watch ran behind, I could always depend on Jill coming outside at the perfect time, which would be eight o'clock in the morning. I wanted so bad to get to know Jill, since I had very few friends, but I could not let down my guard or divulge my secret. I had no desire to go back to prison. I did not want to be the one to have to tell her why I was in prison. So I thought that it would be the best to just stay away from her. No matter how I tried to forget my past, the thought always seemed to creep back in to burn me again and again.

She has now been home for only a couple of weeks. *So far I have been able to avoid her, but there could be a time that we would accidentally run into each other.* Just about that time for that thought to come into my head, I heard someone behind me. "You must be Danny," said Jill. My time for avoiding Jill has come to an end. There was no way of getting out of it now.

Turning around to her, "Yes, I am Danny," I said. Just about that time she stuck out her hand to shake mine "Hi, my name is Jill. I am Amanda Chandler's daughter," she shared with me. "I have wanted to meet you, but every time I start to come up to you, you seem to find something to do elsewhere." Reluctantly, I pulled off one of my dirty gloves to shake hands with her. I knew that I could not be rude to her any longer. As I continued doing my work of cleaning the stalls, she constantly asked me questions about a three-year-old stallion that her mother had bought while she was away. They had named that horse Thunder. The horse had gotten that name because all of a sudden he seemed to get a burst of energy that he would have to display. After about a hundred and one questions on the stallion and on myself, I excused myself to continue my work elsewhere. In the time of her asking questions, there were some questions that I did not know how to answer so by a method that some people call "beating around the bush," I took my best shot.

Later after we were talking, it came to mind after all this time of trying to stay away from Jill; I did not need to be afraid of her mother for she must have been told at the beginning of what I was accused of in the past. I do remember her mother saying at the interview something about Warden Johnson sharing with her the whole thing, but by now does Jill know? It seemed like being in prison; fear always wants to haunt you on just about anything.

In my chat with Jill, I found out that she had a friend back at school by the name of Jenny. Jenny was her same age, thirteen. Jill was hoping to have Jenny to come for a visit later in the summer. Jill shared with me why she was her best friend. Jenny had a heart the size of Texas. I would later find out how true that was, even though that was where she was from. Also, everyone who came to know Jill loved her for her just being herself.

Jill opened her heart and shared with me some things about Jenny. She told me that at first, she did not know how to take Jenny's quiet, rebellious attitude, even though it was much like hers. You see Jenny and Jill both were from a home that were full of heartaches, trouble, and confusion. The only difference between Jenny and Jill was that Jenny was in an accident. When she was about nine years old, she had an accident riding a horse. The horse lost its footing and fell right on top of her breaking her back, leaving her unable to walk very well. Jenny had to adjust to a new way of living.

Jenny knew that she could stay negative for the rest of her life, but that would not help her adjust to the way she would have to live. With Jenny's accident and their friendship, it helped to open up a new door of endless wonders for me. They came to a conclusion that their attitude did not fit their friendship. The choice that Jenny chose helped her to be so open, free, and willing to be just herself. That choice not only effected Jenny, but Jill soon liked what she saw, making her own decision as well.

Chapter Eight

THE TEXAS-SIZED HEART

J ill had been home for about a month now. She was an amazing young lady. She learned so fast at whatever she was taught, when it came to learning about the ranch. I could hardly believe that she was so young; yet knew and was able to do the work. As Jill was sharing with me about her friend, one of the hired hands yelled at Jill from the bunkhouse, to let her know that she had a long-distance phone call. So off she ran to see who was calling for her this early in the morning.

About that time Pedro came over to me and said that he had heard from some town talk that Mrs. Chandler had only married Mr. Chandler for his money. Mr. Chandler was a unique man and could win just about any trophy, as long as it was connected to horses. What threw things in a different direction happened after a couple of years of marriage. Shortly after the birth of his child, he was killed trying to break a horse. Mrs. Chandler did not want to have the responsibility of the ranch or the child, so she left the ranch up to the hired hands and the child-rearing up to a nanny or to the school system. "What an awful way to treat a home and a family," I shared with Pedro. "How can this be the daughter of Mrs. Chandler that I had heard about? She is so outgoing and talkative," I said to Pedro, still confused.

Soon nothing but yelling, and screaming shouts of joy came from Jill as she ran out of the barn. Then Jill put her hand over her mouth, hoping that her mother did not hear her. Her mother just would not understand. That phone call was from her friend, Jenny. Using their new phone system in the barn to communicate with her friend and later with her mother, Mrs. Chandler had told Jill that Jenny could come for a visit starting next week and stay for two weeks on the ranch. Jenny's visit would be sooner than Jill expected. With this phone system, one can call anywhere on the ranch and get in touch with whomever by only punching one or two buttons and a few numbers. With that, Jill was able to get a quick approval from her mother over the phone about Jenny coming to spend time with her, and that meant the world to her. Even though it was just six days, she could hardly wait for the next six days to pass by for Jenny to arrive.

Chapter Nine

A SHAKE OF A HAND

I n the short time that Jill knew me, she did become my
friend; she just did not know it. I wanted to share with
her the idea that I now had a good friend here. Several
days later, Jill came up to me and asked me to shake
her hand a second time. I looked at her like she had lost
her head. She then commented, "There must be something else going on." Again I gave her that look, like
I did not know what she was talking about. This time
I was even more eager but still reluctant to stretch out
my hand to take hers.

"When I shook your hand the first time, your eyes
and handshake said one thing, and now your eyes and
handshake are saying another. One of my professors
shared a technique on how to tell the character of a
person by what their handshakes and what their eyes

are saying. Usually the handshake and the eyes are to say the same thing, but yours do not," said Jill. With that said, I turned to walk away. I just knew Jill must have felt something that might lead me to have to tell her my secret. With that in mind, I continued to avoid eye contact with her, but I knew one of these days, I was going to have to tell her.

The longer the time that Jill was there, the more she wanted to learn about the horses, the fields, and how to run the ranch; even though she was so young. She must have gotten the love for ranch life from her father. From what I could tell, she certainly seemed not to get it from her mother. Every time she tried to get with me to talk about the operation of the ranch or my life, I would continue to disappear. Jill could not understand why I did not want to be her friend.

One day, I noticed that Jill was nowhere to be found. I thought that maybe she had gotten tired of trying to keep up with me and decided to do her own thing or stick with the other workers to help. Was I ever to wrong! Just about the time I turned the corner to go into the barn, I could tell it was past time to clean the stalls. The odor that the wind brought to my nose through the breezeway of the barn was telling me the story. As I picked up the rake and wheelbarrow to gather the bad straw together, out popped Jill.

As she caught me off guard, my rake went up into the air. Not thinking, it brought back bad memories of prison. There I had to be ready at all times, for you never knew when a prisoner would strike back unexpectedly. When I saw who it was, I had the coldest chills to come across my whole body. *Could I really have hurt her,* I thought to myself? "What are you doing," I shouted, as I questioned her actions.

"I was playing. I wanted to catch you before you ran away, like you always do," said Jill.

"I could have hurt you," I shouted.

"You, hurt me? No way." This time, she spoke in a soft-spoken voice of sincerity.

Prison life was hard, and being innocent made it even harder to explain my actions. I was not going to say anything to her, but because of her persistence and what just had happened, I knew I had no choice but to tell her the truth of why I have avoided her all this time. "Jill, do you have a few minutes that we can talk?" I asked her. With a grin on her face, off we went to the pile of hay bales. As we sat down, each on a different bale I thought to myself, *where do I start? How am I going to tell this child and what is she going to think of me*. "Well. Here goes," I said. With that comment, her grinning smile changed. She looked at me in a very strange way. "I wish I had a better way of letting you know something than just coming out with it, but that is all I know to do," I hesitated.

"Well, out with it," she demanded. As she sat there, she took in all that I told her about my past and the time I spent in prison, she continued to look at me in the same manner without changing her facial expression. It was as if she did not believe or it did not matter to her what I had said. Then there was a long pause while I waited to hear what she had to say.

"Is that so? I do not believe you. The way that I shared with you about the handshake, I believe tells a lot about someone, and it says that you are innocent. In your handshake on that first day when I met you, I read in it, more than you could imagine about yourself. That was why I wanted to shake your hand again. Your eyes were telling me of some sadness, but I believe your handshake said other things. I do not believe that you are capable of doing just what you were accused of," said Jill.

"But, because I have been accused of it, your mother may not want you around me. That is why I have avoided you so much during your time here. If my parole officer were to see you and me together, I could go back to prison with no questions asked," I shared. I was so glad that Jill understood what I was going through. She is a good kid, and I would never want to cause trouble for her or my job. I really liked what I was doing and most of the people that I worked with weren't all that bad, either. I suggested leaving, as not to cause trouble for her or her mother. But what even surprised me more, was her willingness to help me out in my time of need.

"Each morning before I come outside, I will check to see if your parole officer is here," stated Jill. She said that since her mother and she did not get along, my secret was safe with her.

"Because of what your mother, said when I arrived about my parole officer and what the Warden said, I really think she is aware of it already," I said with a slight giggle. She wanted in every way to help me out, so that I could teach her the way of the ranch. With that thought, *I knew Jill was going to be a very special person.*

Chapter Ten

ANIMAL LOVE VERSUS PEOPLE

S hortly before Jill came home for the summer, a filly was born. She was so excitable that all the other hired hands had a hard time just getting close to her. I guess it was a special talent that I had with animals because it was not very long before she let me pet her. Then it did not take too long before she started following me around wherever I went. All the other hired hands thought that I had hypnotized the filly. No one else was able to handle her wild and fighting spirit. Jill's mother refused to let her have anything to do with the filly for fear of her getting hurt.

One day after our connection in the barn, Jill watched me from a distance. She noticed that I had a special love for all the animals that I was caring for. She also noticed that I had a hard time in getting along with the hired hands, and people in general. "You know what Danny? I see how you react to the animals. You have such a soft and tender way with them. Why don't you use that same technique with people? Then your relationship with people would be so much better," shared Jill.

I did not want to admit that she was right, but what she told me that day really seemed so easy. Until she said that, I did not realize how easy communicating with others could be. *So, all I had to do was treat people the way I treated the animals, and my relationship with people would improve.* That thought kept going through my head. As the day went by, I kept thinking about her statement over and over. I knew what she was trying to say; however, there was a big difference between the people and animals. People will talk back, but an animal will not, so putting it into action is a lot harder to do than said. At first I thought it would be impossible, but as I thought about it, the easier it seemed to be. It was just like the white horse named Lucky Seven that Mrs. Chandler rode. It seemed like no matter what Mrs. Chandler did to Lucky Seven, he took it and accepted it as a way of life, even after she mistreated him.

Chapter Eleven

THE FIGHT AMONG FRIENDS

As time went on, our friendship broadened as we learned to trust each other. As we worked together, the six days seemed to pass by quicker than expected. Jill's eagerness to learn made her forget about the phone call with Jenny, meaning this was the day for her arrival.

All of a sudden we heard the horn of an automobile blowing long and loud. We stopped working and looked up at each other. My heart went clear to my toes, thinking that it was my parole officer and here I was with Jill. Soon the idea hit us both; it had to be Jenny, so her name soon became a scream. Jill's eyes got as big as a fifty-cent piece, and off she ran, leaving the barn yelling out Jenny's name. Mary Beth had come through once again for Jill. She had set up the guest bedroom downstairs for Jenny to have a place to stay these two weeks.

Seeing those two girls relish their friendship, arm in arm, it took me back to a time, growing up. It reminded me of what true friendship was all about. I had a friend named Barry that I grew up with that lived down the street from me. We did just about everything together. I do not think that I could have had anyone better for a buddy. This great friendship that I had was ended too soon; he was killed in the Vietnam War. With all the screaming, hugging, and laughing that young girls do, I was soon brought back to reality.

With all the noise, you would think that the earth had been invaded. As I rounded the corner, this frail little girl was in a wheelchair. She was so small. When the two hugged, I thought Jill was going to turn over the wheelchair, but she caught it just in time. At that time Jill introduced me to Jenny. It was not long after her introduction that their world opened up to see what they could find here on the ranch. I really think that Jill had in her heart to want to learn the ranch, but with Jenny there, Jill once again became that little girl that she should have been all along.

Out of all the hired hands, Jill chose me to be the one to show Jenny the operation of the ranch. It made me proud, even if it was for just a moment. Jill pushed Jenny around in her wheelchair unless we had to go upstairs, and that was when I carried her. I had already shown Jill a great deal about running a ranch. Jill, being excited about ranching, wanted to show it all to Jenny. It would soon be time to show Jill other things about the ranch. There was so much to teach her. There were things that I waited on showing her like the paperwork, how to plant the seeds in the fields, harvesting the grain to be eaten, or the gathering of the crop, but with her friend here, as of now the right time or season was not at hand. It would all have to wait.

Part of my job was to care for the many animals that they had. Besides the cows and horses, there were animals that they raised for food to go on the table. There were rabbits, chickens, squirrels, and ducks that I had to care for, which took up a great deal of time. The reason for the great amount of time spent away from my duties was for me spending time with the girls, but I didn't mind it. I think Pedro volunteered to to the job while I was away with other duties. The learning process for killing and preparing of the animal for food is one thing, and learning how to raise them is another thing. I think the part of processing the animals for the table was the hardest of all for Jill's soft and tender heart to accept. "I think I will leave that up to the hired hands." Jill admitted. And I agreed.

The time that I had to teach Jill about the ranch soon ran out. I was brought again back to reality, hearing the giggling and laughter from the girls. Jill did just about everything with Jenny here on the Ranch. Some of it was with me and some was with other hired hands. I guess I did not want to admit it, but it was kind of nice to have a break at being the teacher. Not only that, but I was expecting my parole officer to show up soon. I was hoping that Officer Bains would not show up during the time of one of my lessons with Jill.

One morning Jenny came out of the house using her crutches, and entered the barn where I was working. Since it was still early, I asked in a teasing manner, "Where is your shadow?" All of a sudden I realized that Jenny seemed to want to be serious about something. "Mr. Danny, did Jill tell you how I got hurt?" Jenny asked. Jill had told me of how she got hurt, but I wanted to hear her version.

"No, Jenny, and please, just call me Danny. You make me feel so old when you call me Mr. Danny," I said.

"Okay, Danny," she said with a smile. "As I was practicing with my favorite horse, Major, I was doing some pole-jumping. Poor Major caught his foot on one of the poles causing him to fall, landing right on top of me. I must have hit my head on something, causing me to be unconscious for several days. When I finally awoke, it was too late for me to see to my horse. He evidently had broken a leg, and they had already put him down. I did not even get to say my goodbyes to him." As she paused to catch herself, she continued. "So to make a long story short the fall left me crippled, and I was not able to walk very well. I now live most of my new life in a wheelchair or on crutches.

There were several phases that I went through, just like everyone else with the same problem. When you come to a certain point in your life, you have to make a decision. That decision is to how you will allow God to use the crisis in your life. Will it better your life, or will you let the event destroy your life?" Jenny said, sharing with me what Jill had shared with her. She continued telling me how they met. When I met Jill, she was the one that told me that I could let my problem destroy me, making my life miserable. But Jill would not let that take place. You see, she was the one that helped me to see life in the way that I do now." I knew she was right and I knew what I had to do, so I chose to use it to benefit my life in whatever came my way." The question, I had asked myself in the past, of knowing how Jill was brought up was how Jill does what she does and still have the joy and love that she displays, is now answered. They both are remarkable young ladies.

Chapter Twelve

THE SPECIAL GIFT

The first day that Jenny was here, she had fallen in love with the horses. She wanted so badly to ride one of them that it was written all over Jenny's face. No matter how I tried to convince Jenny to try to ride, she turned me down. It was not until the second day that I tried to place Jenny in the saddle. Her body would not do anything but slide to the side, requiring me to catch her before she hit the ground. No matter what we did, Jenny invariably would slide right out of the saddle. I saw how hurt Jenny was. Because of her physical condition, if she was going to be able to ride with Jill, Jenny was going to need a special saddle to help hold her in an upright position. I think they both had the same amount of love for the horses.

I knew I could not give up in finding a way for Jenny to ride for Jill's sake. With Jenny and Jill's hearts broken, off they went to find something else to do. Finishing up my work early gave me more time to think up an idea before the sun was to set. I knew how much riding meant to Jenny, so I knew if I thought hard enough, I could come up with an idea that would allow Jenny to ride the horse of her choice. I had heard of a type of saddle for people that could not walk or stand. It was designed with a high back for them to lean against and multiple straps to help hold the person in place as to not let them slouch, causing them to slide out. Lying in bed as the night continued on, I was contemplating so hard, it felt like my head was going to pop.

About half way through the night, God came through for me. The idea woke me from a deep sleep, not allowing me to return, so I looked for a pencil, wood, and lots of leather. Once I started working, I did not want to stop, so I continued to work all night. Before I knew it, a small ray of morning sunshine came through the small window at the top of the barn. I knew that meant that a new day was beginning, and I was not quite ready. I knew I had to put things in high gear to finish it up. I just knew I had to.

About two hours had gone by when I heard the girls come outside. They were asking each other what they wanted to do today. I knew just how to answer that question for them. As I heard Jill pushing Jenny in her wheelchair nearby, I stepped outside and waved to them to come in my direction. First I told them, "Good morning." I could hardly wait. "I have something that I want to show you two." I was so eager to show them.

As they turned the corner into the barn, Jill and Jenny were so surprised that they could hardly say a word. "Cat got your tongue, girls?" I thought they forgot how to talk. I looked at Jenny to see her reaction and on her cheek was a tear. That tear, was a tear of joy. As she finally spoke, the words could hardly come out. "Where did you get that?" Jenny muttered.

"I made it," I said.

"You like it," I asked?

"Like it? I love it! Now I can go riding. I never have been able to stay on a horse after my accident. My parents would not allow me to, thinking that I would get hurt worse then what I was already," said Jenny.

Now with tears of joy flowing down both cheeks, she rolled her wheelchair over to me, grabbing my hand to give it the biggest hug it has ever gotten. "Well, shall we try it out," I asked? After saying that, the girls had the biggest grins on their faces. So I grabbed the saddle, blanket, and bridle, along with what we needed, then we headed for a horse.

"No! He is mine. I am going to ride him," Jill shouted. The girls went back and forth on who was going to ride Chico. Before I knew it, what I thought was a true friendship seemed no more.

I asked Jenny to excuse Jill and me. We went off to the side. "I thought she was your best friend," I told Jill.

"She is," said Jill.

"Do you not want her to have fun while she is here?" I asked.

"Yes, I do want her to have a good time." said Jill.

"I do not think that she is using her handicap only as an excuse to get her way, do you?" I asked.

"No, I do not think that," shared Jill.

"You know what? Jenny is only going to be here for a short time. I know she, too, has fallen in love with Chico like you have, but she wants to ride him. Since she is only going to be here for only a short time and you will be here for a much longer time, why don't you let Jenny ride him? You will have plenty of time to ride Chico," I shared with her. So, as true friends that they really were, Jenny was allowed to ride Chico that day.

As we finished straightening out the confusion and trying to put Jenny on Chico, I saw Frank over by the corral. "Frank, can you help me for a second?" As I asked Frank for help, Jill and I looked at each other and smiled, knowing now that I had put into action what we talked about earlier about talking to others. I was not sure if I would be able to get Jenny up on the horse. I did not want to hurt her. Besides it is about time that I stopped trying to do everything for myself and get involved with other people.

With Frank's help, we finally got her up in the saddle. She could not stop grinning from ear to ear. I know the saddle must have felt strange. It looked strange with the high back for support and all the extra straps that it took to help hold her in. "How does it feel? The saddle I mean. Are you going to slide out?" I asked.

"It feels great! Mr. Danny, I mean Danny. Sorry. I do not think that I will slide out," Jenny said. "I can't thank you enough for all the hard work and time you have put into this."

I sure felt so insecure about the saddle. "I am not sure if this will hold you the way it is supposed to, so do be careful. If you feel like you are slipping, you get yourself back here on the double. No hesitating, okay? I mean it. You need not to be gone more than an hour.

Okay?" She still gave me no response. "I need for you to come back after one hour so I can check to see how it is doing, and then you can go back out if you want to. Okay?" I insisted on a response to be sure she heard me.

"Okay," she reluctantly agreed.

I asked them to not go beyond the west gate in the pasture next to the house for now because I certainly did not want them too far in case something did happen. So off they went in one direction, and off I went in another. Before I knew it two hours had gone by. I thought to myself, *I hope they are okay*. All kinds of things went through my mind. First, I thought that they both were having such a good time that they did not want to come back, then maybe they were having trouble. The more I thought, the worse I imagined. I was afraid that I was going to have to go out and look for them. I asked some of the helpers if anyone could have seen them come in and I just missed them, but none of the guys saw them come in. As I had made up my mind to go look for them, saddling up a horse, I heard one of the workers yell. "The girls are back." With a sigh of relief, I now knew what it was like to be a parent.

"I thought I told you to come back in one hour," I told them angrily due to fear that something had happened to them.

"Please Danny; do not be mad at Jill. It was my fault" said Jenny. "I was having such a good time, and I did not want to come back," Jenny pleaded.

"I told you that you could go back out again. I just wanted to make sure everything on the saddle was working the way it was supposed to. Besides you could be out there somewhere lying on the ground hurt and not able to get back." I did not mean to be so harsh with the girls. I just hated my new friends to get hurt. Today, I have noticed kids just wanting to do what they want to do and forget what is being asked of them. "You okay?" I asked "Yes, I am and I am sorry for not listening to you. I won't do it anymore, I promise," Jill and Jenny both said at the same time. The girls made a promise that they both tried to keep for the two weeks that Jenny was there. If it was anyone that I felt sorry for now, it was for the horses. The girls rode them every day from sunrise, to sunset.

Chapter Thirteen

THE ACCIDENT

With summer half gone, it was almost time for Jenny to return to her home in Texas. The girls had the best time of their lives, helping all of us hired hands with the ranch work. They both amazed me at how much love they really did have for this place, even at their young age. Jill was doing almost as much as the hired hands were doing in the work area. As time went on, Jill ended up winning over Thunder, the horse that we had been talking about with all those one hundred questions. With her sweet innocent heart, she probably could have just about won the heart of any animal that she had in mind.

They both grew to love working with, being with, and caring for all the horses, even though Jenny could only do so much. Chico became both Jill and Jenny's favorite horse. In Jill, I could see some of her mother's beauty, but she had to have a lot of her daddy's spunk in her, too, because her love for the horses and the ranch was just too great. I enjoyed watching Jill and Jenny riding Chico, working with Thunder, and sometimes Lady as they left the barn each time. I felt a little jealousy, for I knew they could go wherever their heart's desire led them. It was as if Chico, Thunder, or Lady could read each of Jill and Jenny's heart and soul and shared their feelings. I think the horses would miss the girls as much as I will when it was time for them both to return to school.

One day as they were leaving through the barn door, Chico feeling perky, starting galloping too fast. The farther up the hillside Chico and Jenny went, the faster he opened his stride until he reached a full run, speeding over the many hills.

On this new day, Jenny's feeling of freedom would have a high price to pay. Jenny decided to take Chico off to another direction without talking to Jill first, and she was leading the horse into danger. This time it was in a territory into which they had not ventured into before. What Jenny did not know was that I had shared earlier with Jill about the new fresh sharp barbed wire fence I had put up the week before over by the creek, in the direction Jenny was heading. I guess Jill did not have enough time to tell Jenny, either. I knew if Jenny continued in the pace that Chico was running, it would not be long before she would come in contact with the new fence. It would tear Chico up on the impact, as well as Jenny. I could not let that happen to either Jenny or Chico. When Jill saw the look on my face, she realized my reason for fear. Before I could grab a horse, she jumped on Lady, hoping to catch up with Jenny before it was too late. Since she took Lady, there was only one other horse for me to use, Thunder.

So far Jill was the only one that had ridden him; I was not sure how he would respond to me as the rider. As I climbed on, we took off. It was as if Thunder might have also understood what I feared. I do not think I have ever seen Thunder run as fast as he did that day. He must have known something was wrong and was willing to help. Not wanting to even think about all that could happen to either one of them, I began yelling at the top of my lungs as I rode. I was hoping that Jenny would hear me and slow down. No matter how hard or how loud we both yelled, she just continued riding, not knowing what was ahead. With Chico being Jill's favorite horse, I knew that I had to be there this time for Jill. No matter how much I cared for Thunder, I just had to be there for my best friend, Jill.

As Thunder flew over the land I was starting to catch up with Jill. I was praying that none of us hit a prairie dog hole causing anyone to go down. As Thunder and I were nearing the creek, we came across some small brush-like plants. Knowing that they were thorny, I had to have Thunder slow down. I know Thunder did not mean to, but as he was cutting through those bushes, he almost made me fall off. Grabbing Thunder's mane even harder, I hung on for dear life. As I got through the small bush line, I saw that I was too late. For down on the ground Jenny and Chico were lying. Jill had managed to arrive before me. I know she wanted to see if Jenny was alive, but as I dismounted Thunder, I told Jill in a slightly loud voice, "Do not pick her up. Let her stay on the ground. Then I lowered the volume of my voice. "She could be seriously hurt." Lowering the volume in my voice was for not wanting to frighten Chico.

As I started to take a look at my new friend's lifeless form, I wanted to cry for her. Then I noticed one of the leather straps had come loose this time, saving her life. It was because of the loose strap and her limp body that she was thrown away from the horse as he went down. As I brushed a lock of her golden hair from the side of her face, she came to. "Chico! How is Chico?" she asked about her horse. I was so worried about Jenny that I had not even checked on Chico. Jenny was the one that thought about Chico.

"Wait, are you okay," I asked? About that time, I noticed that there was a cut on her forehead. "Stop! You have a cut on your forehead. Look at your arms," I shouted, as she started to crawl over to Chico. Thank goodness, they were just scratches. Wanting to see about Chico, Jenny insisted on trying to crawl the distance over to where he was, so that was when I picked her up to help carry her over to Chico. Chico was really cut up bad by the new wire.

I was glad that I was the one to find him in his condition. If someone else had seen Chico, they might have suggested having Chico put down because he was hurt so badly. I could not see it happen a second time for Jenny. That was what had happened to Jenny when she had her accident besides taking a long time for her to recuperate. I did not want that to happen again for Jenny. Plus, it could mess up the friendship with Jill because Jenny was riding Jill's horse. I knew I had to get him back to the barn to start working on him before he went into shock. That is, if he could even be helped.

In the process of examining him, I saw that there was a big gash across his chest where the wire caught him. His right foreleg had a big gash and several small cuts, as well. Once I got him loose from the wire, I started thinking, *how would I get him home?* was my next and biggest question? I told Jill that I needed to go back to the house to get medical supplies and help. She told me that she was willing to stay with Jenny and Chico while I returned to the house. That was when Jill realized that I rode Thunder. "Thunder, you're a good boy! Do for Danny what you would do for me." I knew Thunder would listen, so that took the fear out of what he might do unexpectedly.

Once again I was going to have to run Thunder as fast as he could go back to the house to get help. When I arrived, Pedro must have seen me ride to catch up with the girls. Since he was not sure if I had caught up with them in time, he had a similar thought that I might need some items for an accident. So, thanks to a good foreman, not too much time was wasted. I knew Thunder could not make one more round trip, and even if he could, we needed the old truck to bring Chico back home. In heading back to the house, I also figured if I had enough helpers, and the right equipment, we could put the horse on one of the small flatbed trailers to bring him home, since Chico was small in size.

Pedro, thinking ahead once again, came through as a good foreman. Beside the supplies, and the home-made crane that he had gathered, Pedro also had attached a small trailer to the old truck and was ringing the alarm bell for helpers. Part of country living was when you needed help, everyone who could manage to get away would drop what they were doing and come running to help you. While waiting for the helpers to arrive, I shared with Pedro that Chico was worse off than Jenny. "She has some cuts and bruises and tomorrow she will be sore, but she is all right." It did not take long for the bad news to spread, so as the help gathered, we then took off to where Chico and Jenny were waiting.

I told Don since he was squeamish about blood that he did not have to help. I gave some instructions to him about preparing the barn for a place to put Chico. With him being new to his job, I was hoping that he would know what to do about the barn; besides there was not much time left with the sun about to go down. Concerning Chico, I did not know how long it would take to get him on the flatbed trailer and did not want him getting a chill lying out there on the cold ground.

By the time we arrived to the scene, the sun had gone down. As we arrived to where Jill, Jenny, and Chico were, the car lights shown down on them. By now Jenny was sitting up on the ground with Chico's head in her lap. Jill and Jenny, sitting on the ground in the dark, showed no fear for the possibility of wild animals coming to check her and the injured horse out. The only fear that Jenny had was for her new friend, Chico.

As Pedro and I drove up in the old truck, all the helpers jumped out of the back of the truck early as not to scare Chico. They got into a huddle to talk about how they were going to use the equipment that they brought to get Chico onto the flatbed trailer. Pedro went to check Chico over to see how bad he really was. The gash was large and deep, but I knew what was going to have to be done when it came to caring for him. There would be some sewing, but first he must have an antibiotic shot, shave the hair around the cut, wash the cut out, and put some antiseptic spray on it. It is hard to believe that such a little wire can do so much damage. I had seen a horse cut up before by barbed wire, but not this bad. However, it all was going to have to wait until we got Chico back to the barn.

Pedro and I quietly approached Jill and Jenny, hoping not to scare Chico. We needed to share with her about what we were going to do to get Chico home. At that point, Pedro took over. I knew that whatever we did, it would need to be done fast. At that time Jenny sat up again to hear what I had to say. I told her that the crew and I would do everything possible that we could to take care of him. It was hard for both of the girls to smile, but they knew I meant what I said.

It took all the strength of the six guys and the equipment to put Chico onto the flatbed trailer. I am glad that Pedro thought of the trailer and supplies ahead of time. The ranch just could not operate so smoothly without Pedro. With the truck being high off the ground, there was no way that we could put Chico in the back of the truck.

When we got back to the house, Matt, one of the hired hands went and got Jenny's wheelchair for her to sit in. With Jenny's love for her new friend, she did not want to leave the barn. I told the girls, "If you stay out of Pedro's way, he probably would let you stay for a little while." Pedro did let them stay for a little while. I was beginning to see how amazing the two girls were together. "There are a few more things that I have to do to the truck, don't stay too long." I said. So I left the barn to finish removing the things in the truck that we took with us. When I finished, I looked at my unfaithful watch to wonder if it was correct or how much it was off in time. Not really caring about my watch, I knew that some time had passed, or should I say way past their bedtime.

Walking into the barn I shared, knowing it would break their hearts, "Jill and Jenny it is way past your bedtime. Pedro would give his best care to him throughout the night. If you would like to say, "Good night to him, you may." Very reluctant Jill leaned over and gave him a kiss, while Jenny just waved as she sat in her wheelchair. They did as they were told and went inside. I really do not think that the girls got much sleep that night. I know I didn't.

We took Jenny to the doctor the next morning to have her checked over. She tried to tell us she was fine, but we wanted a professional opinion. "See, I told you I was okay," Jenny said. They cleaned her up and gave her a few words to be more careful next time, and then we went back to the ranch.

Jill was not only a true friend to Jenny, but to Chico, as well. I had not been in the barn long when Jill came in. This time, she came into the barn way before sunrise to check on Chico. Jill had a favorite blanket that she brought with her. She had brought it out to put on Chico in hopes that it would help him feel better. As time went by, she showed me through her actions that no matter how old or young she was, Jill not only wanted to become but was capable of becoming the new owner and leader of her father's ranch someday.

As Chico was mending, the time came that Jenny was to return to back to Texas. Jill did not want to see Jenny go. They had so much fun being kids and pretending to be responsible adults with the ranch. They soon said their goodbyes and gave each other their hugs, and she even gave me one, too. Just before Jenny got into the taxi, she asked if I would write to her. This time it was my turn to be reluctant, so I nodded my head and said that I would try.

Yes, after Jenny's first accident on her horse, she could have made any decision she wanted on how to live her life, but I think she definitely made the right decision. She is one "dynamite" of a young girl who will go far in life.

Chapter Fourteen

THE DECISION

Time had passed, and with Chico getting back to his old self again, Jill gave me an unexpected big surprise. Just out of the blue one day, Jill came to me with a very unhappy face. This was about the only time, besides when Jenny left, that she did not have a smile on her face all summer. I did not know what to think. Soon Jill came over to me to talk. "Danny I need to talk to you. I know that I am only thirteen years old, but I think I have found what I would like to do for the rest of my life," shared Jill now with a twinkle in her eyes. "Summer is almost over and I have a problem."

"Yes, what is your problem," I asked?

"Mother wants me to go back to school and then to college to be a lawyer. Being a lawyer is the far-thest thing from my mind. You and Pedro have showed me a good bit at how to run a ranch, how to break a horse, how to work the fields, and so much more. I know that there is more to than just working outside when it comes to running a ranch, and I want to learn. You both have been the ones to show me what my love in life really is. Since you gave me the opportunity to have the responsibility of caring for Chico, you have opened a new door for me. I want to take over the ranch for mother and the dream that my dad once shared with my mother when I was a baby," Jill said.

I just stood there and listened as she spoke, taking in all what she had to say. I could hardly believe all the excitement that rose up in her voice as she continued to share everything with me. With what little bit that I knew about her, I do believe in my heart that she was right. I do believe she had found her dream in life, and of all choices she could make, she chose to be the owner and operator of this 3,500-acre ranch called "The Chandler Ranch." That would be a big responsibility.

I have been amazed at how Jill had come to learn and do what she has done in such a short time. For her to be so young, her wisdom was so great. I thought that if I showed her other things than working outdoors, like the paper work and the blood and guts of the vet's office so if an animal gets hurt, she might change her mind, but I was the one to flunk the test, not her. The time when Chico got hurt proved that I was wrong in that area. No matter what I did to discourage her, it only made her that much stronger and more determined to follow through with learning the value of a dollar and the selling of a horse that it took to be a true rancher. I continued to sit and listen to what she had to say. I just needed some time to think of how to answer her.

"I do not want to be a lawyer! Will you talk to mother and convince her that I want to run the ranch instead?" begged Jill.

"I do not know if I can do that. You know how she is when she makes up her mind about things," I reminded Jill. I guess I was really trying to convince myself, more than anyone. "Remember, I have this problem of speaking to people. For some reason the words just won't come out," hoping to convince her otherwise to forget asking.

"Remember, all you have to do is act like you are talking to one of the horses, and with the kindness in your heart and not thinking that she will say no, maybe she won't." Jill was really working hard to win me over. I finally agreed to give it a shot. So off to the house I went to see what damage I could do. O-o-ops, not damage, but good I can do. *Yeah! Good. Think positive,* I spoke to myself, putting one foot in front of the other.

Just before I vanished into the house, looking back, I saw Jill pacing back and forth outside the barn. It was not too long before I was heading back to the barn. With the short amount of time, I guess Jill must have thought that the answer was to be a definite "no." I guess Jill could not take what might have been said, so she headed into the barn to be with Chico. As I returned, she hit me with her words. "What did she say? Will she let me stay and learn the ranch?" Jill was very eager in finding out the answer.

No matter what I tried to say or do, Jill saw right through me. I could not hold it in any longer. I broke out into a big grin. Soon we both broke out into laughter. She was overjoyed, and almost broke my neck as she hugged it. There was only one condition that Jill was going to have to follow through with, and I was not sure that she was willing to do it. You see, Jill wanted to stay and not return to school. She wanted to do it now.

"It took some talking, but she agreed to let you become the operator of the ranch; however, you will have to go to college and earn a business degree so that you will be able to operate the ranch correctly. You should be about around twenty by the time you finish."

I shared with Jill. She did not like the idea, but she was willing to accept it since the ranch would be hers someday.

It seemed like the easiest talk that I have ever had with Mrs. Chandler since I started working here. Maybe if I need to talk to Mrs. Chandler again, I will do that again—talking to her like I was talking to a horse. That idea from Jill really worked. I guess you are never too old to be taught by a thirteen-year-old.

Chapter Fifteen

THE TALK OF THE TOWN

Not knowing how it got started or when it happened, talk about me was now all over the little town of Pottersville, Arkansas. Since it is so small, it did not take very long for any news to get around. I really do not think that Pedro or Jill had anything to do with the spreading of the gossip. What was the gossip? I was now accused of stealing one of the bags of grain for the horses from the ranch. I guess if it really comes down to it, I could leave and go somewhere else to fight it out; however, I figured that if I left I would have to be on the move fairly often anyway, as long as I notified my Parole Officer.

The next morning, Mrs. Chandler called me into her living room. "What is this that I have been hearing from the town people," asked Mrs. Chandler? Someone had spread a rumor of me taking some grain from the barn at the ranch. Now I am having a second accusation against me, and neither one is true. When someone has gone to jail, they are the first ones to be blamed when a crime had been committed.

I believe the next few words that I was going to have to share would be the worst words that I would have to ever say in my entire life. I thought Mrs. Chandler had already been told about my past, but no matter what I said, she would not believe me. Not really being aware of Jill's presence, Mrs. Chandler asked me to pack my things and leave. As I was about to leave, Jill came out from behind an open door. "You can't let him go. He couldn't have taken the grain. He is too important. Between Pedro and him, this has become a wonderful ranch." Just about that time, Jill lowered her eyes and took a big swallow to say, "If you let him go, then I will go back to school, and never to return to this place again." insisted Jill.

"I thought you wanted to take over this place someday." stated her mother.

"I do, but not if you are going to send Danny away," reassured Jill. I knew that their relationship was not very good, but I wanted to be the last thing to come between Jill and her mother. Jill finally convinced her mother to keep me, due to all what I had done for the ranch, saving Jenny's life and Chico's life, as well as, what I had taught Jill about ranching.

It seemed, every time I went into town, the people seemed to snub me more and more. It got to the point that I really did not want to go into town any more. By now everyone knows that I served my time, and now they're accusing me of something else. And don't forget about "Hatchet Hammer, my parole officer."

What I did not know at that time was that one of the children from a family that lived next door to the Chandler Ranch had wandered off into the mountains, and the rumor was that I had taken her and might hurt her. So now this was the second thing I was being accused for. I had only been thinking about myself along with how frustrated I had become with the town people. The more I thought about it, the more my frustration grew to lead me to decide to leave my new home and what few friends I had made. Seem like no matter what I said or did I could not convince the people of Pottersville, Arkansas that I was innocent of my previous crime, and that I had not taken this little girl or stole the bag of grain. I still had paid my time; much less I would not hurt anyone.

121

Not wanting to leave without saying goodbye to my dearest friend, Jill, I wrote a quick note to thank her for all her help. She had become a true friend to me. I did not want to cause any more trouble between her and her mother and the town. So I packed up a few things and slipped out the back door of the bunkhouse, leaving the note, and headed over the hills. I was praying that no one would see me as I left. Once again, that horrible feeling of being empty and lonely crept up on me. It had been a long time since I had felt that way.

Because of not wanting anyone to see me leave, I did not turn on my flashlight until I had made it up into the closest hill. The moon was so full and beautiful that night that it lit up most of the way for me. I felt that I must get as far away as I could, so I walked until my feet did not want to go on any longer. This was the first time in months that I did not even think about my parole officer and what she or the government would have done if they knew that I had left on my own.

At first all I wanted to do was just get a short distance from the house, but for some unknown reason the soreness of my feet did not compel me to stop. They kept on insisting on going farther and farther. I was not sure why they insisted on going, so I just went on with them and their funny feelings leading the way.

As I was going through some brush, I heard something. The noises in the wilderness are so different than the noises that were in prison. Out there, I really was not prepared if I was to come in contact with a wild creature. I stopped to see what it could be. They have so many wild animals here that the noise could be from any kind of animal. As my heart began to pound in my chest, the noise got louder and louder. I almost was afraid that if I breathed any harder, a wild animal would hear me and know that I was close to it.

As I stood there breathless, the bushes continued moving. I stood as still as I could. Just about that time I saw a little hand as it pulled back a branch. Then I knew what was causing the rustle of the brush. It turned out to be Ashley. Ashley was the four-year-old little Davenport girl who lived on the edge of Mrs. Chandlers' 3,500-acre ranch. But what was she doing out here? Was she the little girl who had disappeared into the mountains? Her home happened to be miles away. That must have been why I had to keep on going. If I had stopped, we never would have come across each other out here in the woods. She could have died out here.

When Ashley saw me, she came running up to me with her eyes full of tears running down her cheeks. I keeled down to scoop her up into my arms. Being so tiny and frail, I was surprised that she had made it this far from home. I reassured her not to worry— she was safe, and nothing was going to hurt her.

With her now in my arms, we walked a little farther to an open area. Now that it was almost midnight by the moon being straight up, I did not think they were still looking for her. I thought the best thing to do was to start a fire for both of us to get warm and to discourage the wild creatures for at least this one night. At first, I had the thought of going on, but what was I going to do with her? Then I knew I had to be the one to take her back home to everyone in that town. I hated to have to hear what they were going to say. I was just praying earlier for a way to prove to them of my innocence. This may be just the way to do it.

I knew that the one tin can of food that I brought with me would be just right for Ashley and me, for after tonight we would not need any more. I placed it into the fire just long enough to warm it up. Ashley did not know of anything else to say, but "thank you" for saving her life. Just about the time that I pulled the can of beans out of the fire, I turned to see why she had stopped talking and noticed that she had fallen asleep. As I tucked her in for bedtime, using my bedroll, she managed to wake long enough to say once more, "Thanks," with an ear-to-ear grin on her sleepy-eyed face as she fell fast asleep.

The night seemed to pass quickly. As the sun came over the horizon, I threw dirt and my leftover water on to what was left of the coals. Then I woke up Ashley so that we could start our journey back to town. With it being a long time since my son was small, plus being in prison, I had forgotten what it felt like to have the hand of a small, helpless little child in mine. It reminded me of innocence, helplessness, and the needing an adult to help guide her back home, so I was going to do just that.

The walk back down to the town was long, so as she became tired, I held her in my arms once again. We were about half way down the mountains, when we saw half the town heading our way. As I woke her, I still was holding her in my arms. Her daddy was in front of the group. When he saw her, he came running, yelling out her name. When Ashley heard her dad calling out her name, she pulled her head up, and began to squeal and squirm. Down to the ground she quickly went.

At first her dad, Mike, did not know what to say or do. He had mixed emotions. At first he acted as if he was to take a swing at me, but little Ashley yelled to her dad to reassure him that she was all right and that Mr. Danny did not hurt her. As a matter of fact, she told her dad and everyone there. "Mr. Danny is a nice man. He found me. I was lost and couldn't find my way home." After she said that, the group of town people came over and started patting me on the back, except Mike Davenport, Ashley's dad. I found out that day, it does not take a chain link fence to keep someone out; words or actions could do the same harm.

I really have not ever liked getting recognition for something I had done, so I used that as an excuse to start back to town. As I took a couple of steps, all of a sudden I felt a dainty, soft hand, grab my little finger once again. As I looked down to investigate, there was the biggest grin of sunshine on Ashley's face. She was telling me that the people were now saying that the whole town accepted me. Now, I was hoping I could actually enjoy where I lived. Maybe having to prove myself was over or was it just a puff of wind? Because of this one guy, Mike, not wanting to accept me, does that mean I would have to move on? In the back of my mind, I felt that either I was going to have to constantly prove myself to the town people because of Mike, or I could make it easy for everyone by just moving on. The time that I was there, I really did enjoy this town of Pottersville, Arkansas, and I did not want to leave. It now was my new home. I just could not understand why this one person wanted to cause trouble for me.

About that time I looked off to the side, and there was Mrs. Randi Bains, my parole officer. My heart went down to my feet, leaving a pile of rubbish in my stomach. I knew it was all over, now that she saw me with Ashley and the town people. She would not understand, even if she would give me a chance to explain. Back to prison I would go. I expected Randi to push her way through the crowd right up to me and put handcuffs on me. All she did was grin like everyone else was doing; then all of a sudden she put two thumbs up in the air as if to say, you're doing fine. "Go for it," she said, as she turned and walked away.

After so much confusion, I turned to walk in the opposite direction, carrying my bag down the main road of town. I had made up my mind to leave. I heard someone from a distance yelling at me. It was Mike, Ashley's father. My pride told me to just keep on going, but my heart told me to stop. So I listened to my heart. Mike, out of breath from running, pleaded with me not to go. He wanted me to come back and stay.

Mike shared with me that they had found out that Matt, one of the helpers at the ranch had really been the one that took the grain. Oh not for himself but to give to the horses. When the supplies had come in, Matt had taken one of the bags of grain to feed the horses without checking it in on the paperwork. So you see, there was a misunderstanding between the helpers.

What I did not know was that Mike had been wrongly accused of something when he was much younger. When Mike was a boy, his older brother Ben had destroyed a historical marker in the town, which could not be replaced. Mike's brother pointed the finger at him, making the whole town believe that Mike was the one that destroyed it. For some unknown reason, one of the town people decided to give him a second chance. That gave the town time enough to find out that his brother Ben was the real one who destroyed the marker. Now it was Mike's turn, in learning to accept this outsider, and to extend the same hand of love that was extended to him, by giving me a second chance.

We need to know all the facts about someone before we accuse them, because we could be wrong like Mike was.

The End

CPSIA information can be obtained
at www.ICGtesting.com
Printed in the USA
LVOW01s0541140716

495681LV00014B/92/P

9 781498 476096